STAR WARS®

ATTACK OF THE CLONES™

ANAKIN

by Lisa Findlay
illustrated by Scott Kolins

Random House New York
www.randomhouse.com/kids

Official *Star Wars* Web Sites:
www.starwars.com www.starwarskids.com

 Published in the United States by Random House, Inc., New York, and simultaneously in Canada by Random House of Canada Limited, Toronto. RANDOM HOUSE and colophon are registered trademarks of Random House, Inc.
ISBN: 0-375-81506-6

Printed in the United States of America April 2002 10 9 8 7 6 5 4 3 2 1

STAR WARS®
ATTACK OF THE CLONES™

THE SAGA CONTINUES . . . with Exciting New Books!

- *Star Wars: Attack of the Clones Movie Storybook* (0-375-81534-1; $7.99 U.S./$10.99 Can.)
- *Star Wars: Attack of the Clones Movie Scrapbook* (0-375-81582-1; $7.99 U.S./$10.99 Can.)
- *The Stars of Star Wars* (0-375-81603-8; $5.99 U.S./$8.99 Can.)
- *Anakin Skywalker: A Jedi's Journal* (0-375-81594-5; $8.99 U.S./$13.99 Can.)
- *Jedi Training and Trials Quiz Book* with Lightsaber Pen (0-375-81602-X; $6.99 U.S./$9.99 Can.)
- *The Skywalker Family Album* (0-375-81497-3; $3.25 U.S./$4.99 Can.)
- *I Am a Jedi Apprentice* (0-375-81493-0; $3.25 U.S./$4.99 Can.)
- *Jango Fett: Bounty Hunter* (0-375-81464-7; $3.99 U.S./$5.99 Can.)
- *Anakin: Apprentice* (0-375-81463-9; $3.99 U.S./$5.99 Can.)
- *Star Wars: Attack of the Clones Big Sticker Book* (0-375-81595-3; $6.99 U.S./$9.99 Can.)
- *Anakin and Amidala Coloring Book* (0-375-81506-6; $3.99 U.S./$5.99 Can.)
- *Heroes and Villains Coloring Book* (0-375-81507-4; $3.99 U.S./$5.99 Can.)
- *Star Wars: Attack of the Clones Paper Doll Book* (0-375-81508-2; $3.99 U.S./$5.99 Can.)
- *Star Wars: Attack of the Clones Ship Schematics Punch-Out Book* (0-375-81509-0; $3.99 U.S./$5.99 Can.)
- *Star Wars: Attack of the Clones Postcard Book* (0-375-81561-9; $3.99 U.S./$5.99 Can.)

Collect them all!

A LONG TIME AGO IN A GALAXY FAR, FAR AWAY . . .

ANAKIN SKYWALKER, JEDI APPRENTICE

FOR TEN YEARS, ANAKIN HAS STUDIED AT THE JEDI TEMPLE ON THE CITY PLANET CORUSCANT.

ANAKIN WORKS HARD TO LEARN THE JEDI ARTS.

THE FORCE IS STRONG WITH ANAKIN.

OBI-WAN KENOBI IS ANAKIN'S JEDI MASTER.

ANAKIN HAS RECEIVED A NEW MISSION-
HE MUST GUARD SENATOR PADMÉ AMIDALA.

DEADLY KOUHUNS!

STOP THAT DROID!

ANAKIN PICKS UP HIS MASTER!

THE VILLAIN IS GETTING AWAY!

GOOD THING ANAKIN IS AN EXPERT PILOT!

ANAKIN AND OBI-WAN CORNER BOUNTY HUNTER ZAM WESELL!

ANAKIN HIDES
PADMÉ AT A NABOO
LAKE RETREAT.

"ARE YOU GOING TO USE ONE OF YOUR JEDI MIND TRICKS ON ME?"
"THEY ONLY WORK ON THE WEAK-MINDED. YOU ARE ANYTHING BUT . . . !"

ANAKIN TAKES PADMÉ TO HIS HOME PLANET, TATOOINE.

ANAKIN'S STEPFATHER, CLIEGG LARS; HIS STEPBROTHER, OWEN LARS; AND OWEN'S GIRLFRIEND, BERU WHITESUN, ON THEIR MOISTURE FARM NEAR MOS EISLEY

ANAKIN BORROWS OWEN'S SPEEDER BIKE TO SEARCH FOR HIS MOTHER.

ANAKIN LOOKS FOR HIS MOTHER IN A TUSKEN RAIDER CAMP.

OBI-WAN IS IN DANGER! ANAKIN AND PADMÉ FLY TO GEONOSIS TO HELP!

ANAKIN FIGHTS THE GEONOSIANS!

CAPTURED!

ANAKIN: "WE DECIDED TO COME AND RESCUE YOU."
OBI-WAN: "GOOD JOB."

MEET THE REEK, THE NEXU, AND THE ACKLAY.

IDEAS, ANYONE?

SAVED!

YODA HAS BROUGHT THE CLONE ARMY!

COUNT DOOKU WON'T GIVE UP!

ANAKIN SKYWALKER

A SECRET EXCHANGE OF VOWS

WE'LL NEVER GIVE UP!

PADMÉ HAS NEVER BEEN AFRAID TO FIGHT.

"YOU HAVE BEEN CHARGED AND FOUND GUILTY OF ESPIONAGE."

"WE DON'T RECOGNIZE THE REPUBLIC HERE, SENATOR."

CAUGHT!

EVEN C-3PO IS IN TROUBLE.

ANAKIN AND PADMÉ LAND ON GEONOSIS, ONLY TO BE CHASED INTO A DROID FACTORY.

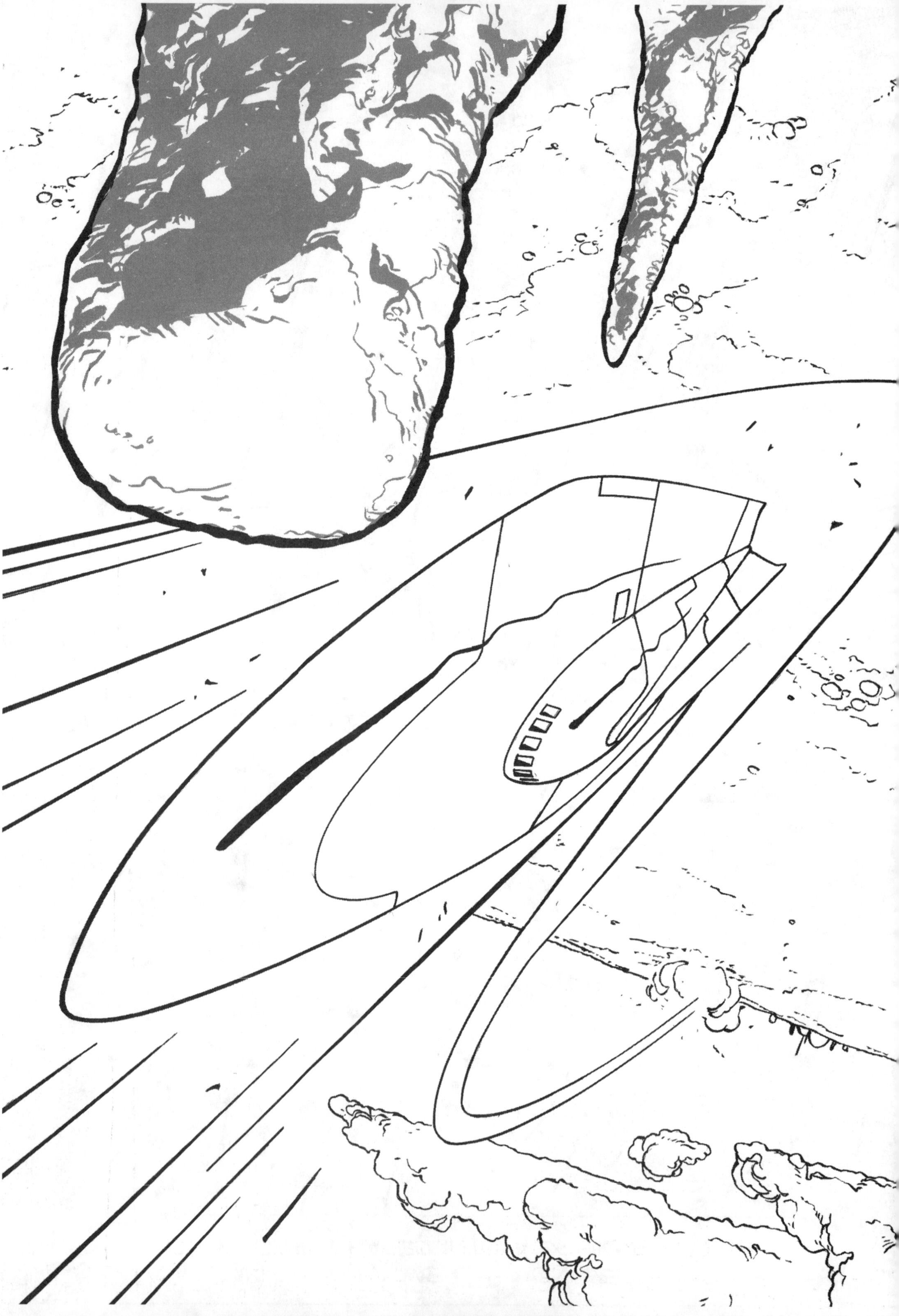

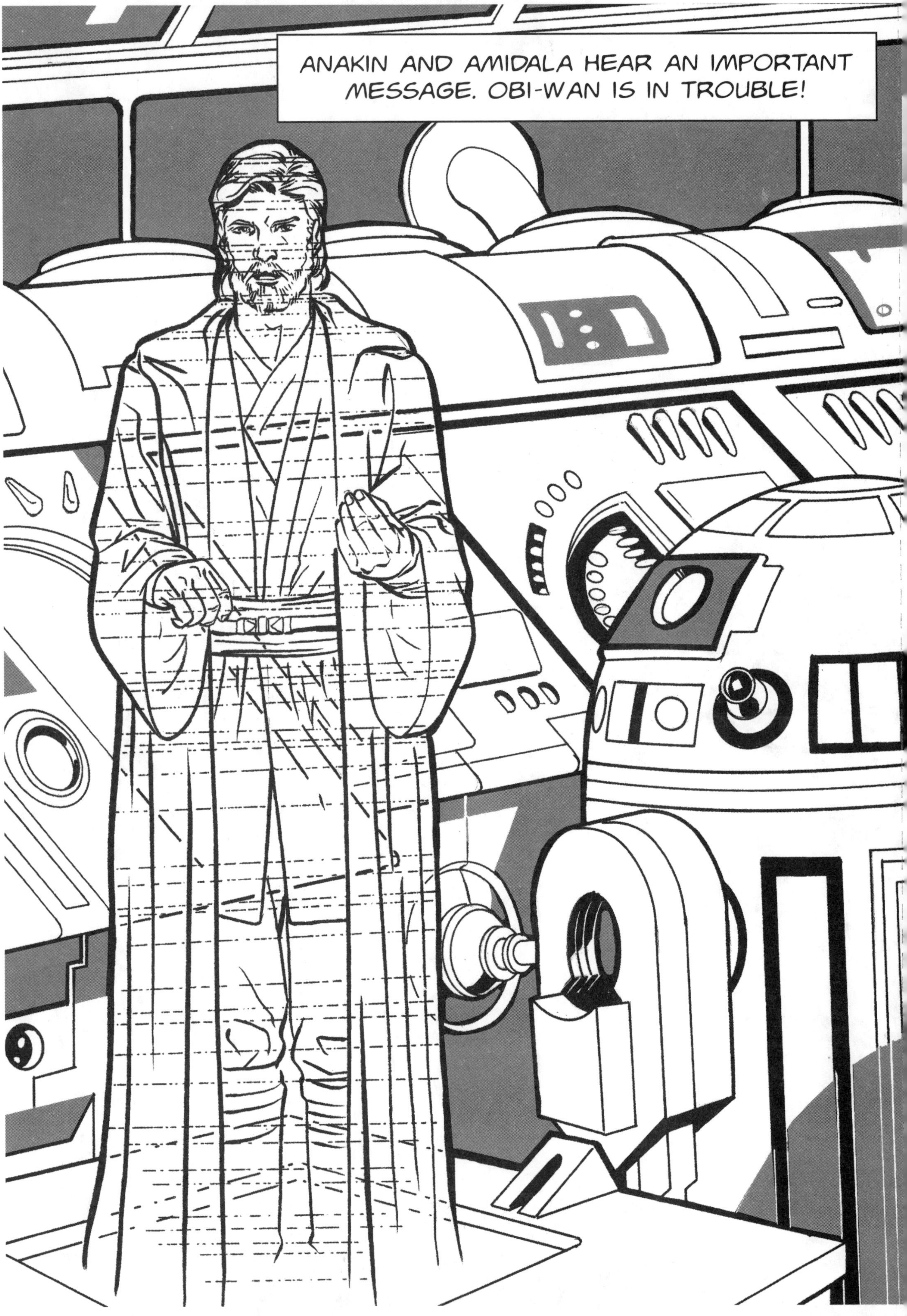
ANAKIN AND AMIDALA HEAR AN IMPORTANT MESSAGE. OBI-WAN IS IN TROUBLE!

THERE IS SOMETHING SPECIAL
BETWEEN PADMÉ AND ANAKIN SKYWALKER.

PADMÉ ENJOYS SPENDING TIME WITH ANAKIN.

AS A SENATOR, PADMÉ IS CLOSE WITH THE CURRENT QUEEN OF NABOO, QUEEN JAMILLIA.

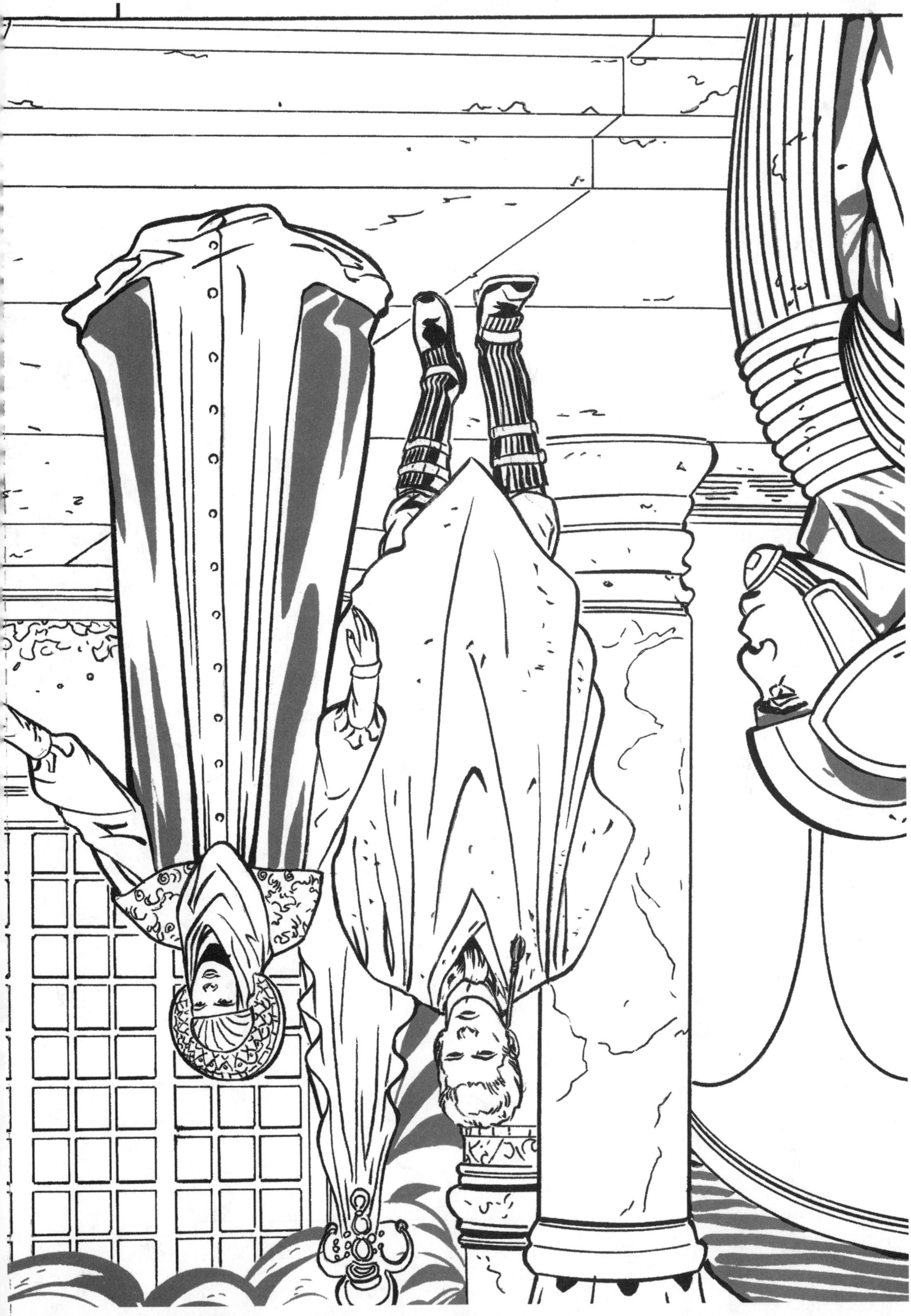

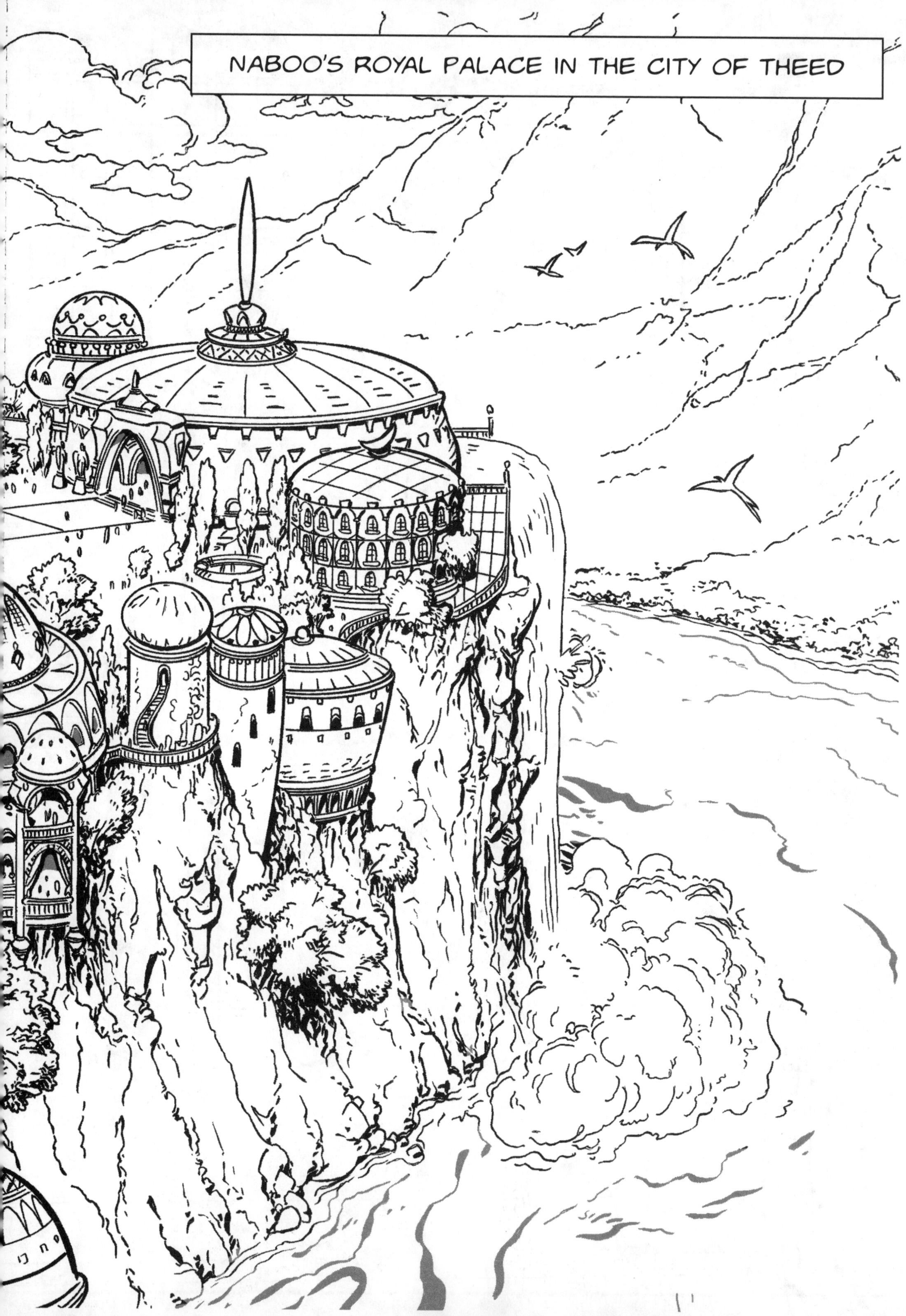
NABOO'S ROYAL PALACE IN THE CITY OF THEED

AT 14, PADMÉ BECAME QUEEN OF NABOO.

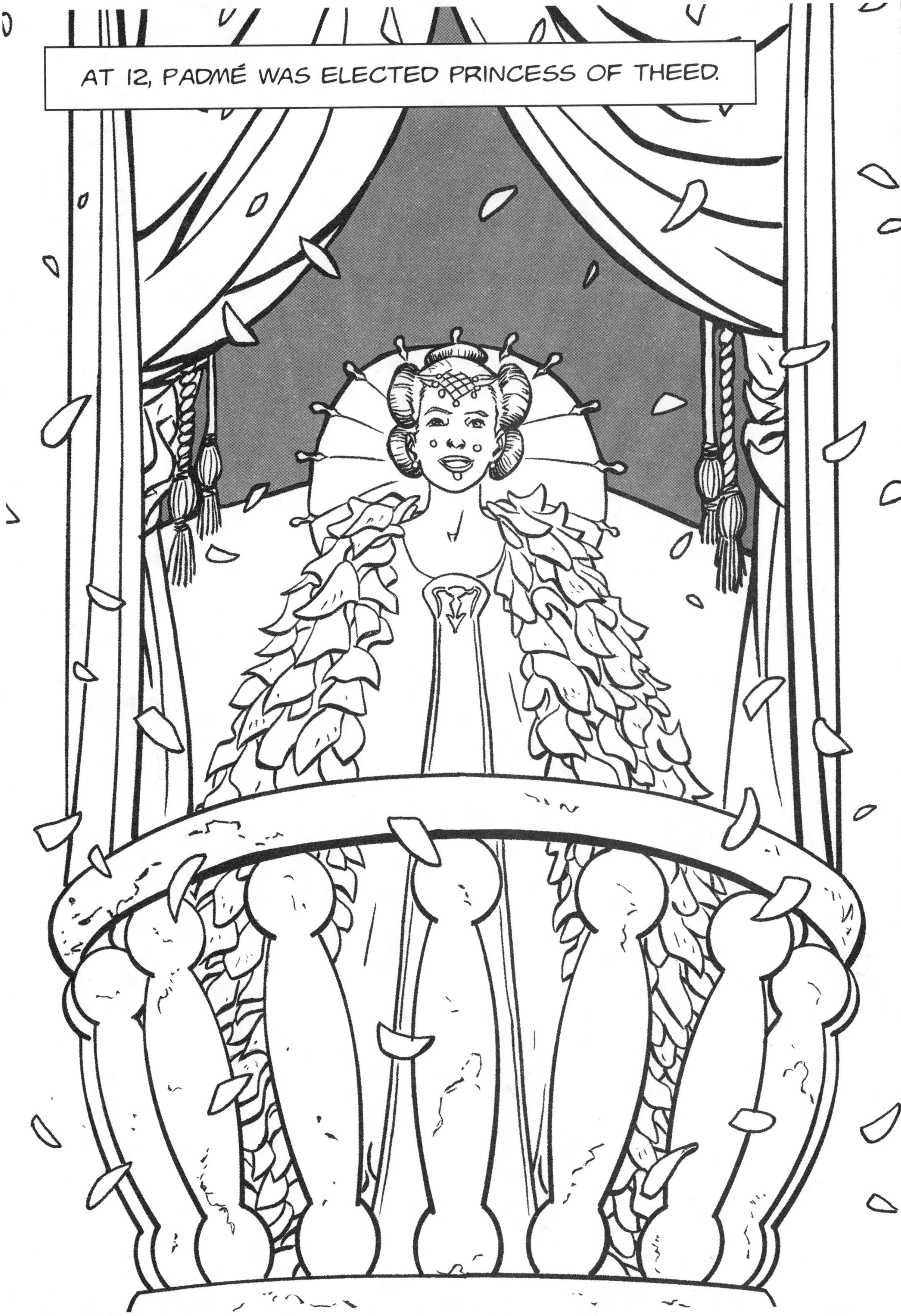
AT 12, PADMÉ WAS ELECTED PRINCESS OF THEED.

FROM THE TIME SHE WAS YOUNG, PADMÉ ALWAYS WANTED TO HELP PEOPLE.

PADMÉ'S FAMILY ON NABOO: MOTHER AND FATHER, JOBAL AND RUWEE NABERRIE; SISTER, SOLA; AND NIECES, RYOO AND POOJA

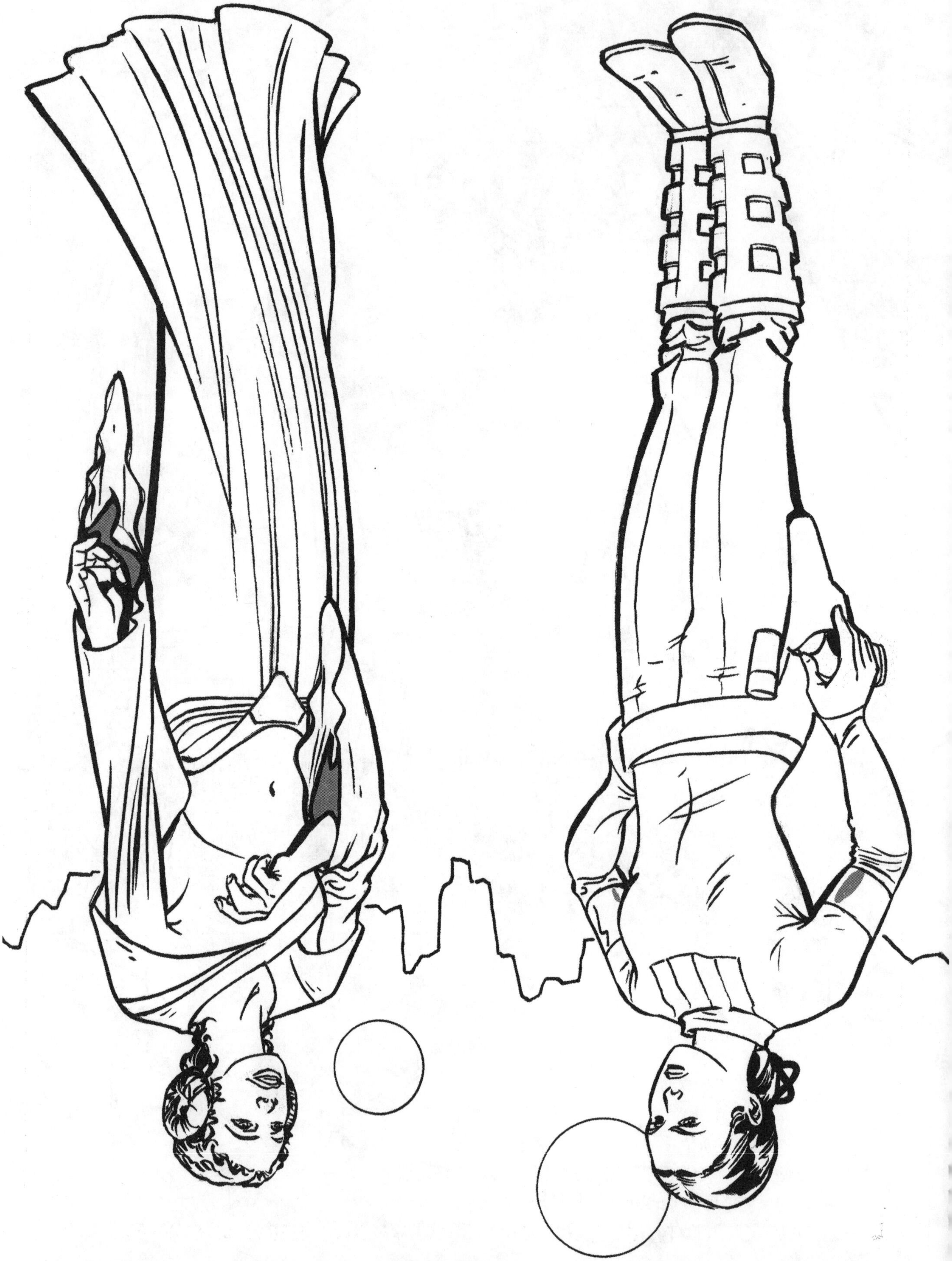

PADMÉ'S WARDROBE ON NABOO AND TATOOINE

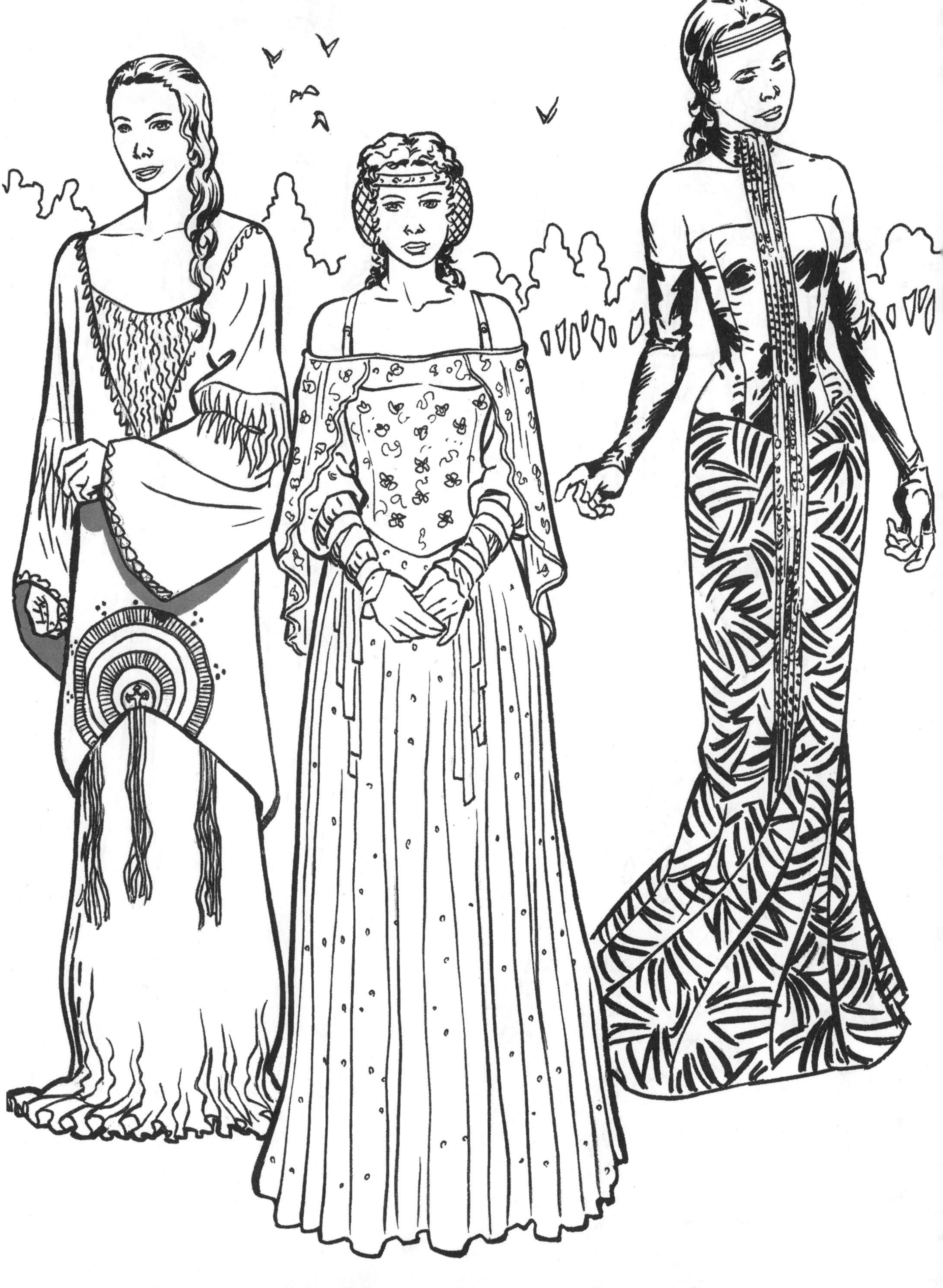

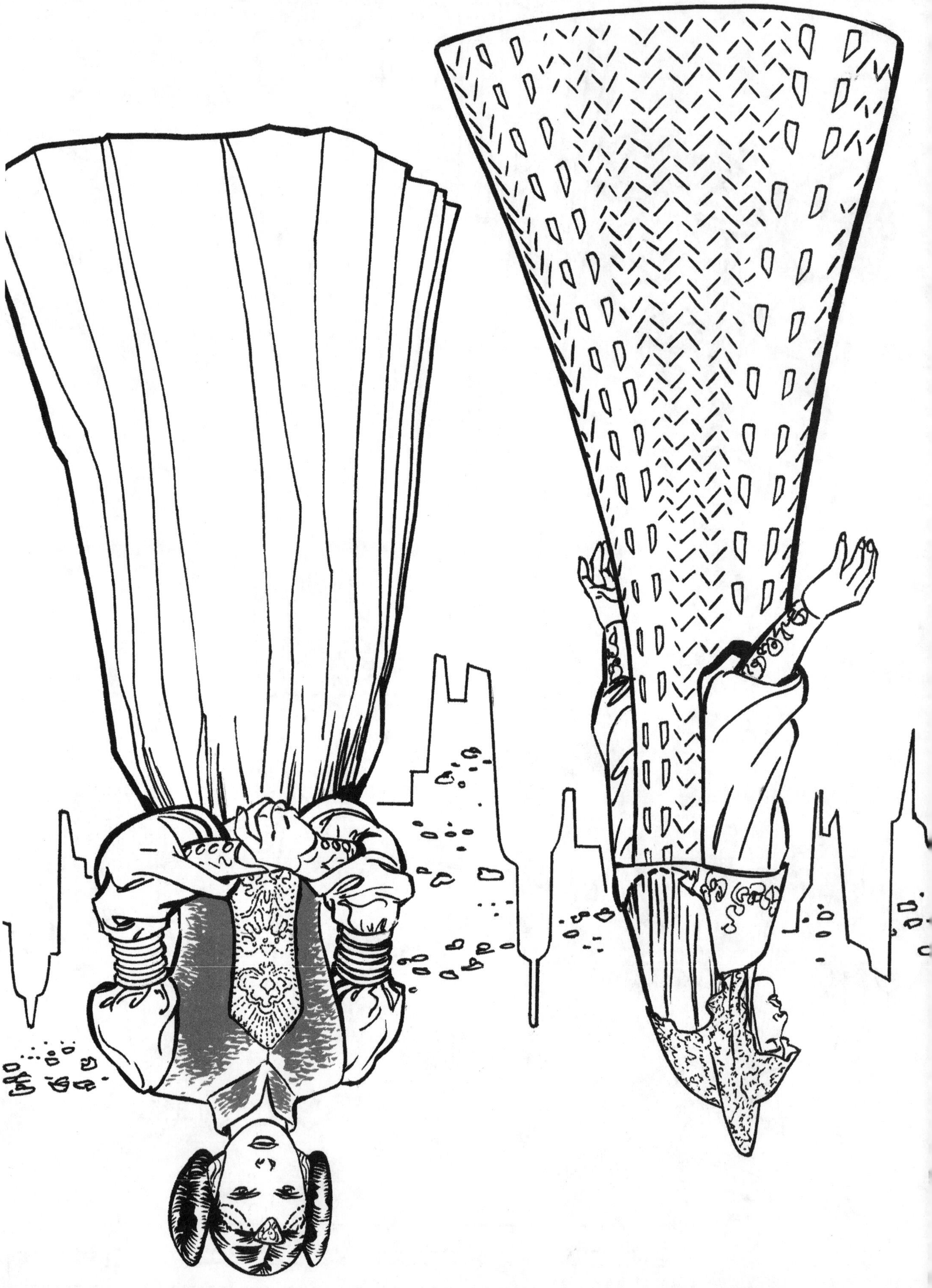

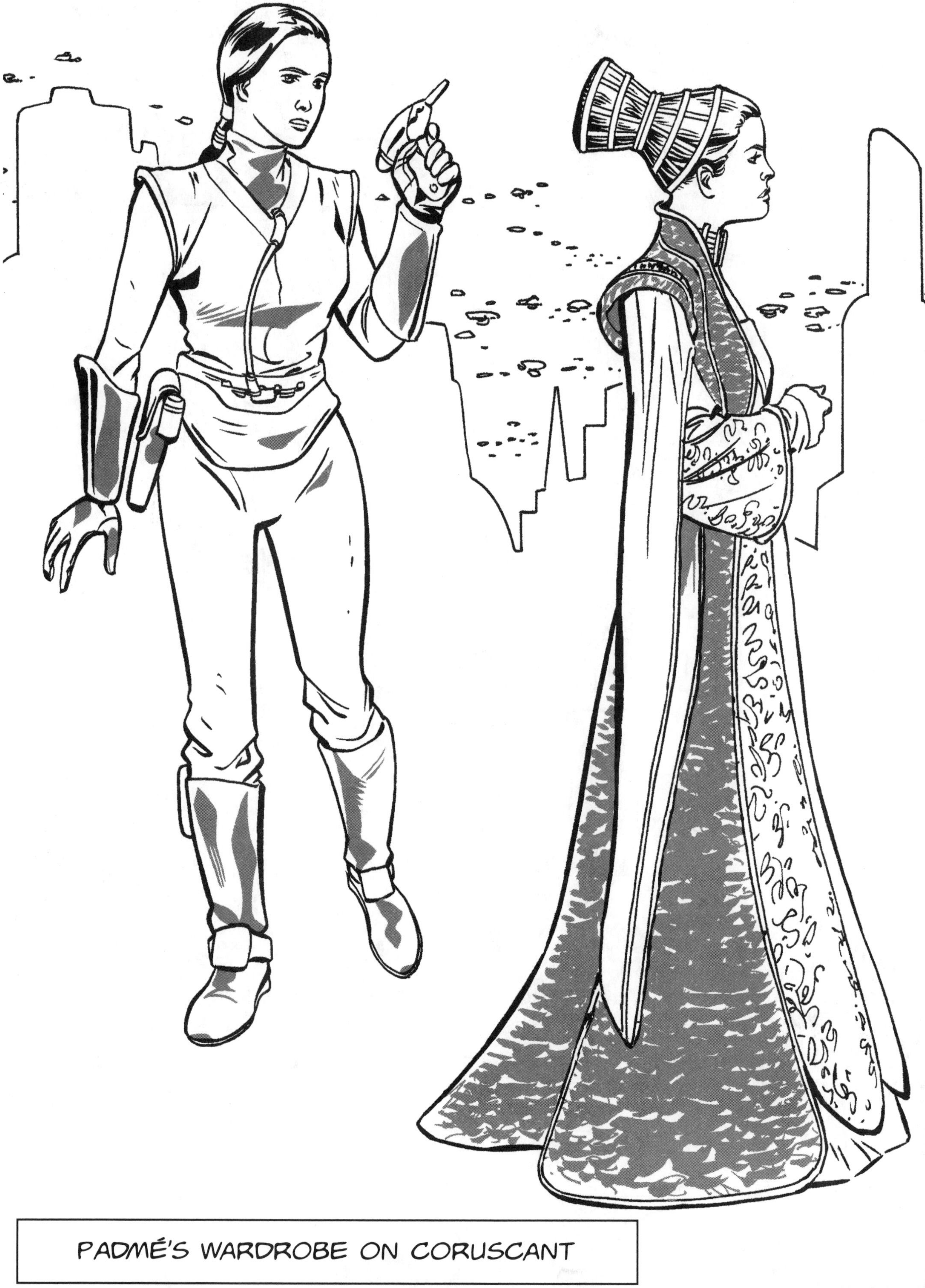

PADMÉ'S WARDROBE ON CORUSCANT

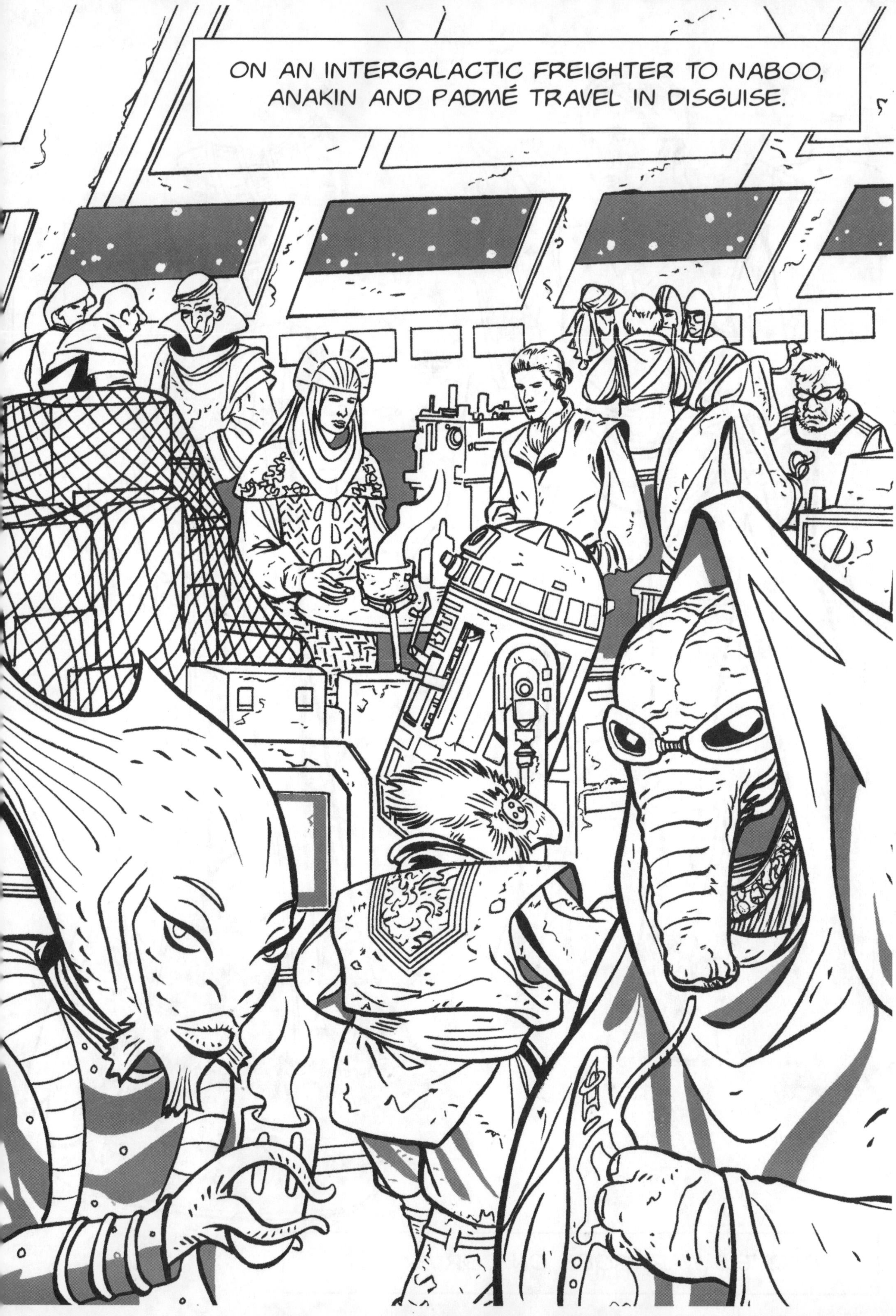
ON AN INTERGALACTIC FREIGHTER TO NABOO, ANAKIN AND PADMÉ TRAVEL IN DISGUISE.

"I DON'T NEED MORE SECURITY. I NEED ANSWERS. I WANT TO KNOW WHO IS TRYING TO KILL ME."

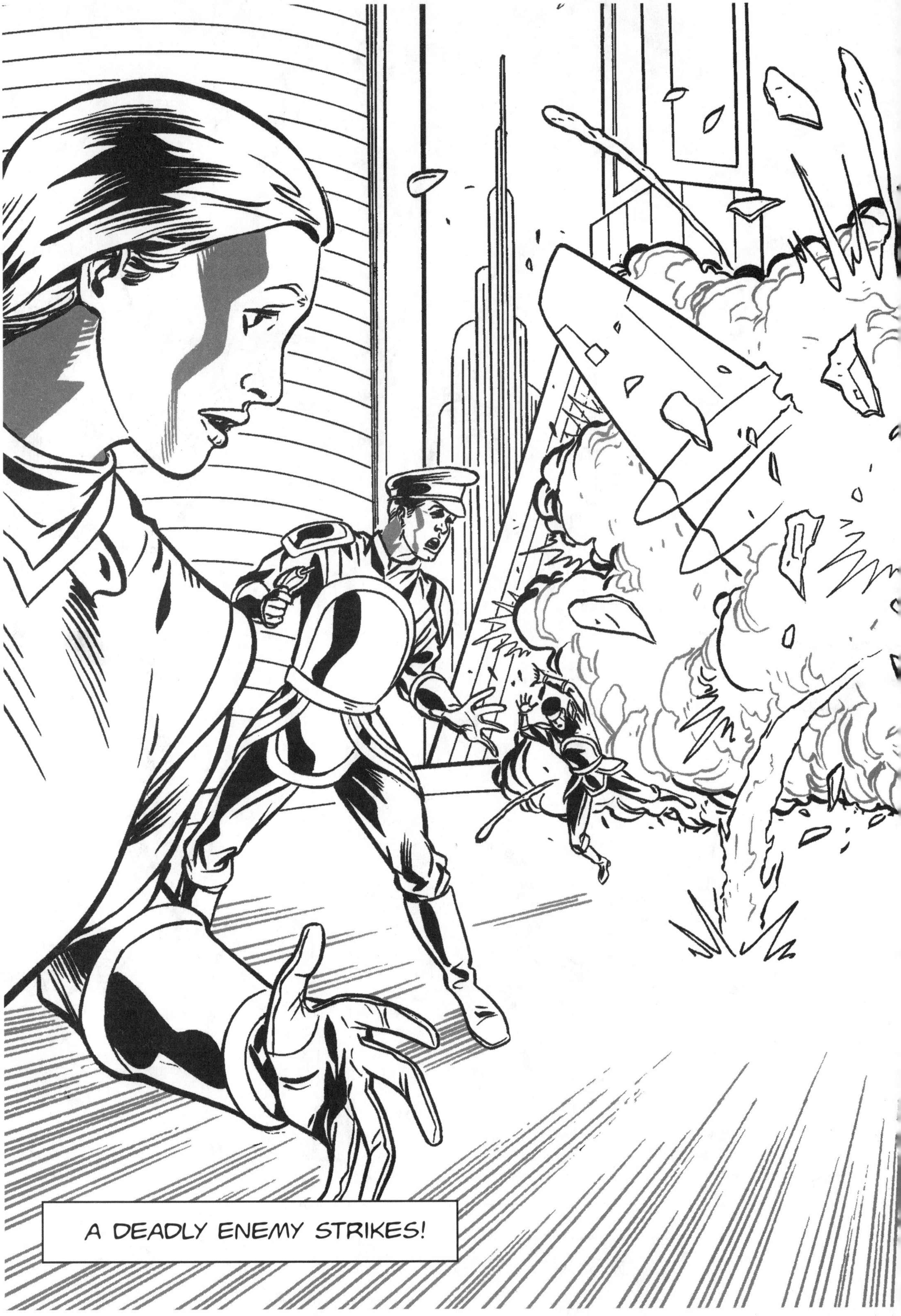
A DEADLY ENEMY STRIKES!

PADMÉ AMIDALA IS NOW A SENATOR.